The House that Jack Built

For Kelly, Joh and Guy – D. M.

Barefoot Books
PO Box 95
Kingswood
Bristol
BS30 5BH

This book was typeset in Clearface Regular 24pt
The illustrations were prepared in acrylics on hotpress watercolour paper

Graphic design by designsection, Frome, Somerset
Colour separation by Grafiscan, Verona
Printed and bound in Hong Kong by South China Printing Company (1988) Ltd

This book has been printed on 100% acid-free paper

Hardback ISBN 1 84148 250 1
Paperback ISBN 1 84148 252 8

British Cataloguing-in-Publication Data: a catalogue record
for this book is available from the British Library

1 3 5 7 9 8 6 4 2

The House that Jack Built

Diana Mayo

Barefoot Books
better books for children

This is the house that Jack built.

This is the malt
That lay in the house
that Jack built.

This is the rat
That ate the malt
That lay in the house that Jack built.

This is the cat that chased the rat,

That ate the malt

That lay in the house that Jack built.

This is the dog

That worried the cat,

That chased the rat,

That ate the malt

That lay in the house that Jack built.

This is the cow with the crumpled horn,

That tossed the dog,

That worried the cat,

That chased the rat,

That ate the malt

That lay in the house that Jack built.

This is the maiden all forlorn,

That milked the cow with the crumpled horn,

That tossed the dog,

That worried the cat,

That chased the rat,

That ate the malt

That lay in the house that Jack built.

This is the man all tattered and torn,

That kissed the maiden all forlorn,

That milked the cow with the crumpled horn,

That tossed the dog,

That worried the cat,

That chased the rat,

That ate the malt

That lay in the house that Jack built.

This is the priest all shaven and shorn,

That married the man all tattered and torn,

That kissed the maiden all forlorn,

That milked the cow with the crumpled horn,

That tossed the dog,

That worried the cat,

That chased the rat,

That ate the malt

That lay in the house that Jack built.

This is the cock that crowed in the morn,

That waked the priest all
shaven and shorn,

That married the man
all tattered and torn,

That kissed the maiden all forlorn,

That milked the cow with the
crumpled horn,

That tossed the dog,

That worried the cat,

That chased the rat,

That ate the malt

That lay in the house that Jack built.

This is the farmer sowing his corn,

That kept the cock that crowed in the morn,

That waked the priest
all shaven and shorn,

That married the man all tattered and torn,

That kissed the maiden all forlorn,

That tossed the dog,

That milked the cow
with the crumpled horn,

That worried the cat,

That chased the rat,

That ate the malt

That lay in the house that Jack built.

Barefoot Books
better books for children

At Barefoot Books, we celebrate art and story with books that open
the hearts and minds of children from all walks of life, inspiring them to read
deeper, search further, and explore their own creative gifts. Taking our
inspiration from many different cultures, we focus on themes that encourage
independence of spirit, enthusiasm for learning, and acceptance of other
traditions. Thoughtfully prepared by writers, artists and storytellers from
all over the world, our products combine the best of the present with the best
of the past to educate our children as the caretakers of tomorrow.
www.barefootbooks.com